For Holden, my wee happy hog—J.C.
This book is for you!—S.W.

Owlkids Books acknowledges the financial support of the Canada Council for the Arts, the Ontario Arts Council, the Government of Canada through the Canada Book Fund (CBF) and the Government of Ontario through the Ontario Media Development Corporation's Book Initiative for our publishing activities.

Published in Canada by
Owlkids Books Inc.
10 Lower Spadina Avenue
Toronto, ON M5V 2Z2

Published in the United States by
Owlkids Books Inc.
1700 Fourth Street
Berkeley, CA 94710

Library and Archives Canada Cataloguing in Publication

Crossingham, John, 1974-, author
Turn off that light! / written by John Crossingham ; illustrated by Steve Wilson.

ISBN 978-1-77147-101-5 (bound)

   I. Wilson, Steve, 1972-, illustrator   II. Title.

PS8605.R684T87 2015 jC813'.6 C2014-908457-9

Library of Congress Control Number: 2015900221

Edited by: Karen Li
Designed by: Claudia Dávila

Manufactured in Dongguan, China, in April 2015, by Toppan Leefung Packaging & Printing (Dongguan) Co., Ltd.
Job #BAYDC16

A B C D E F

Publisher of Chirp, chickaDEE and OWL
www.owlkidsbooks.com

click

TURN OFF THAT LIGHT!

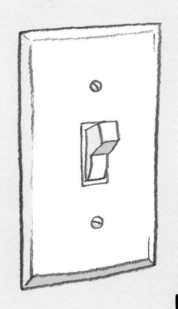

written by
John Crossingham

illustrated by
Steve Wilson

Owlkids Books

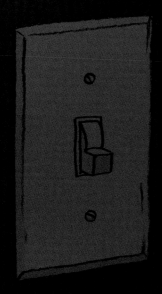

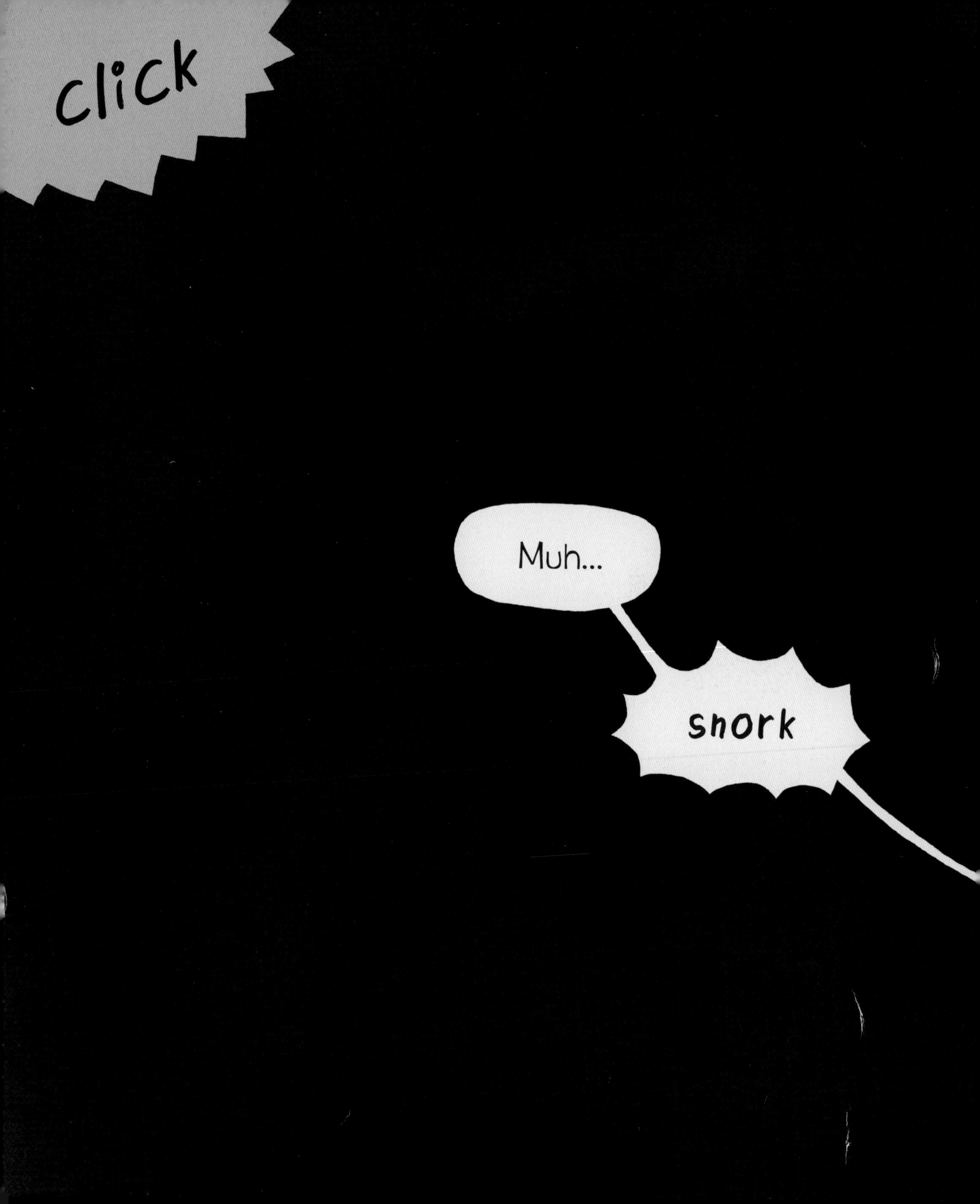
click
Muh...
snork

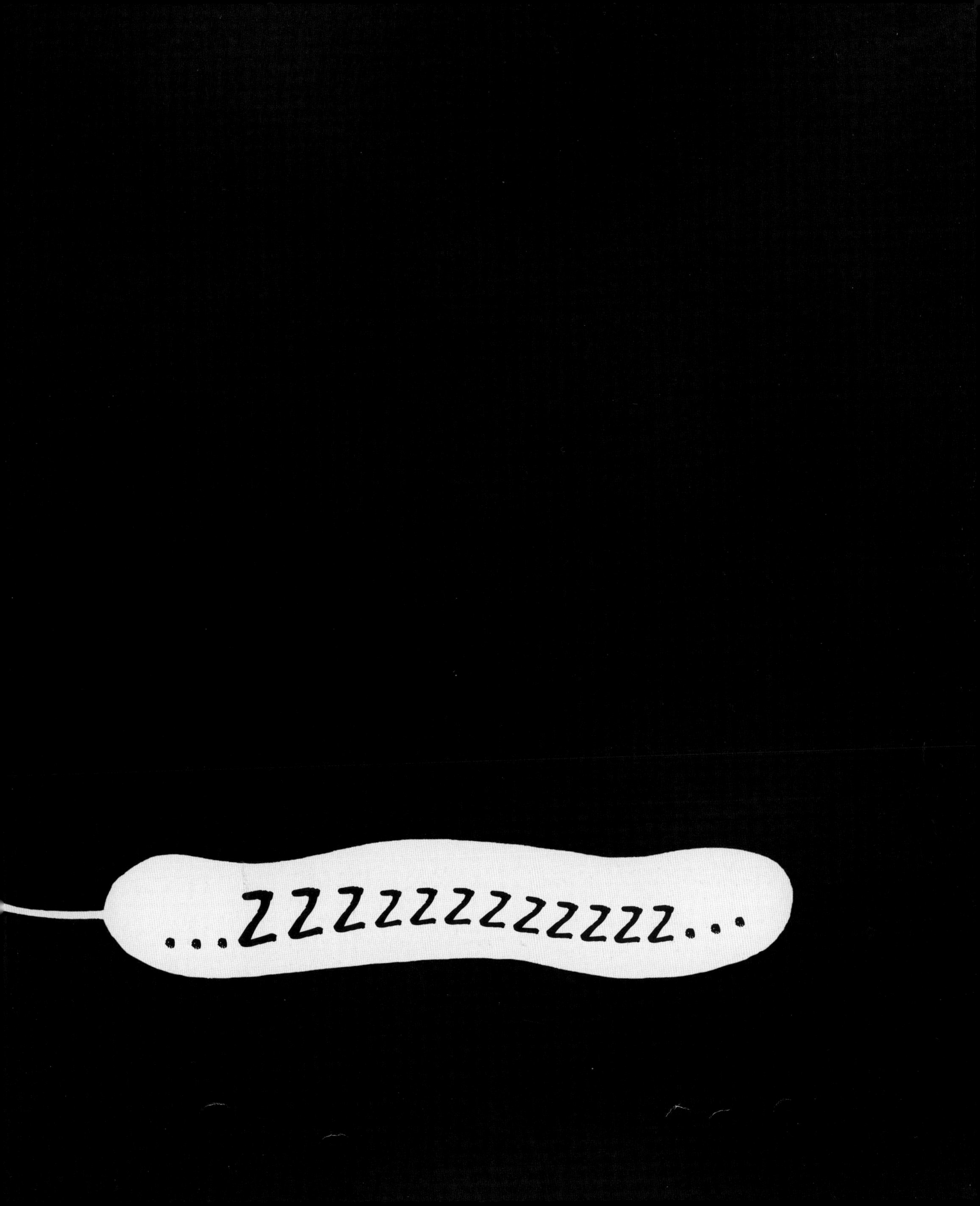
...ZZZZZZZZZZZZ...

click

...you.

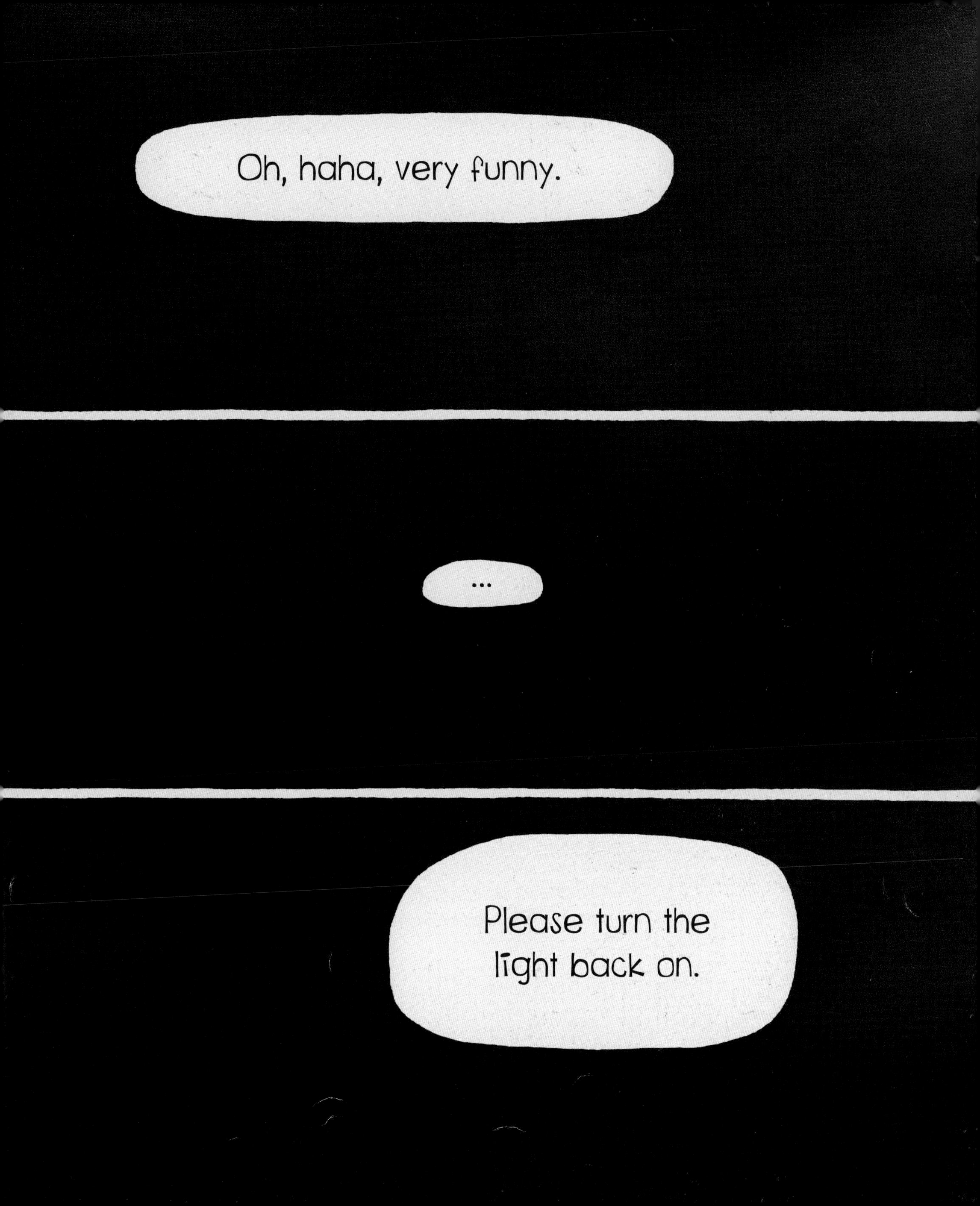
Oh, haha, very funny.
...
Please turn the light back on.

click

There you are.

Hmm... Maybe I'm
being a bit grumpy.

I *was* sleeping...

Ok, let's have a little chat.

I'll just come over there to...

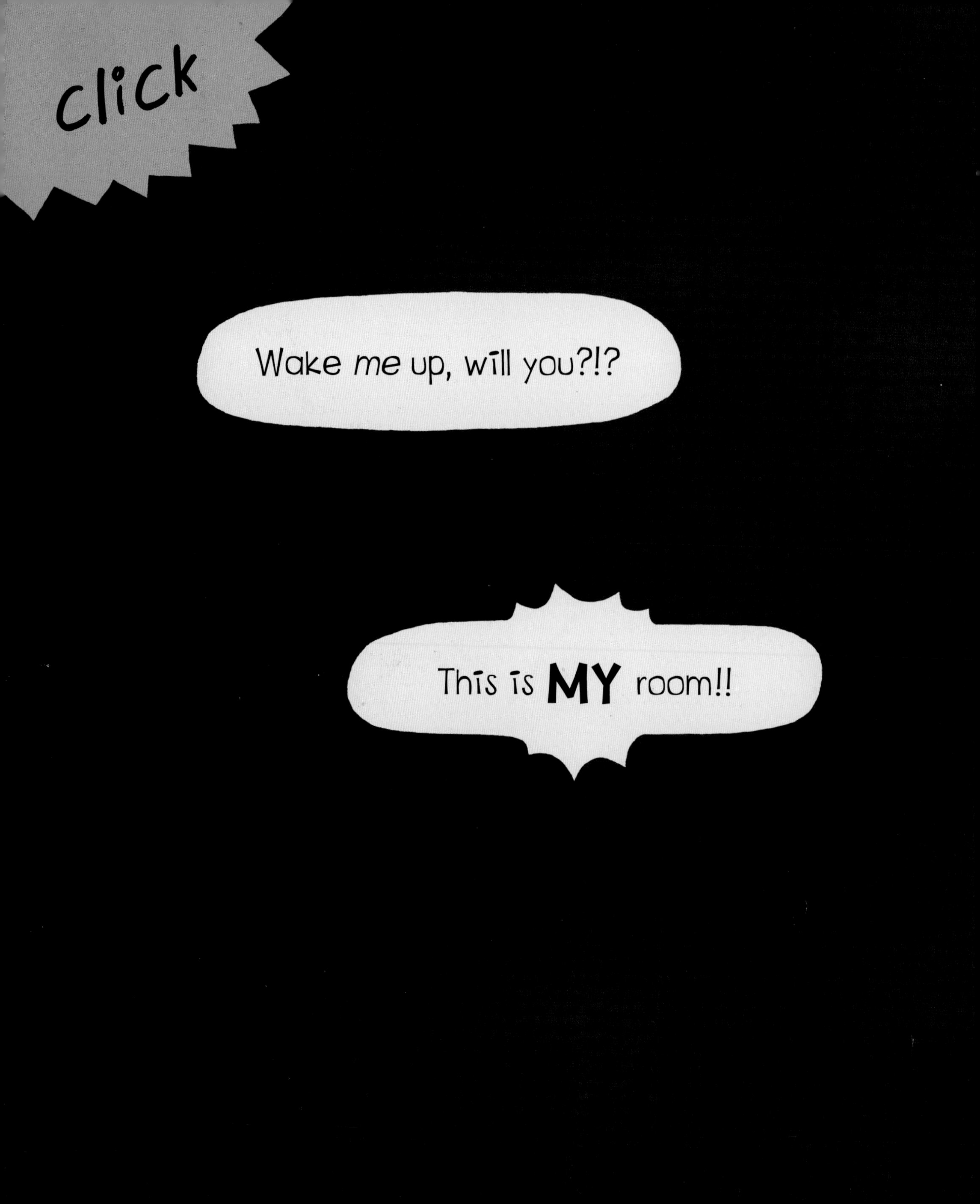
click
Wake *me* up, will you?!?
This is **MY** room!!

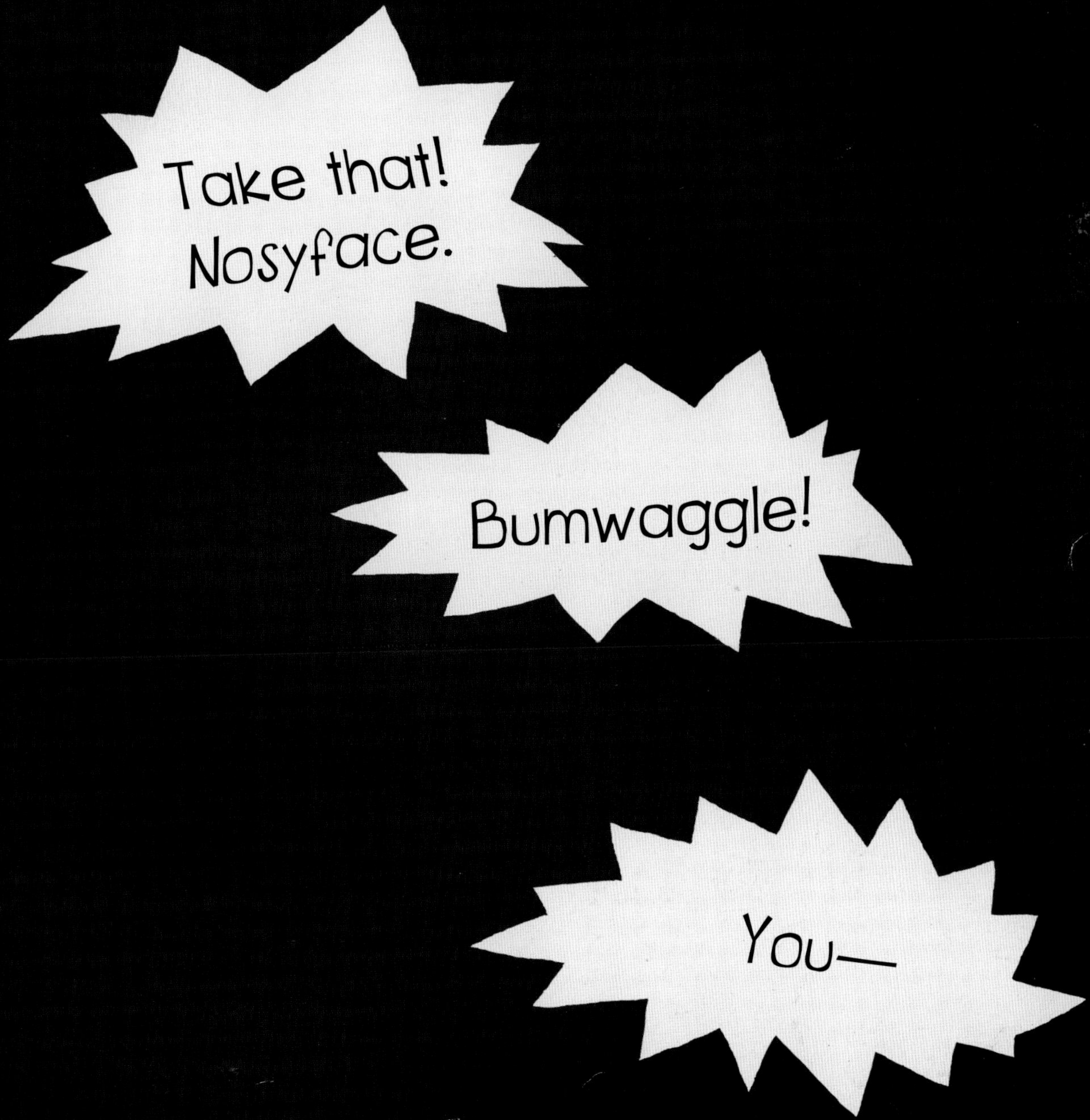
Take that! Nosyface.
Bumwaggle!
You—

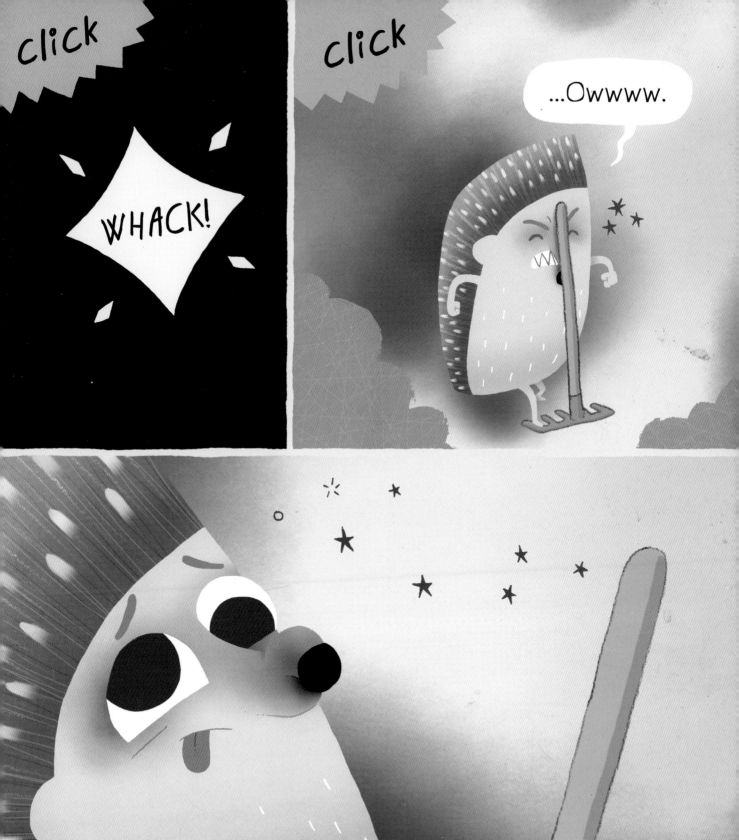

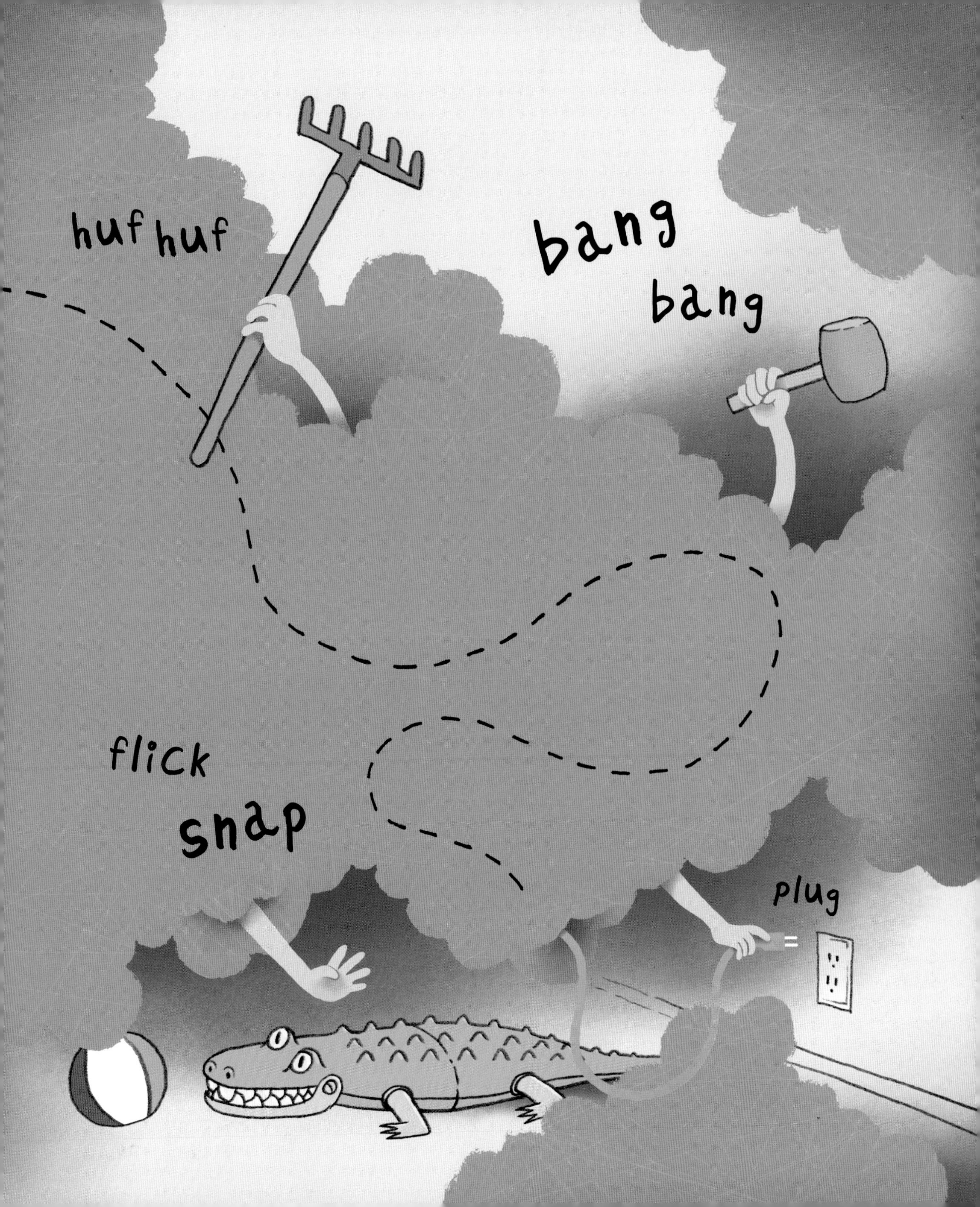
huf huf
bang
bang
flick
snap
plug

click

Hee hee...
Hoo hoo hoo,
heh heh...

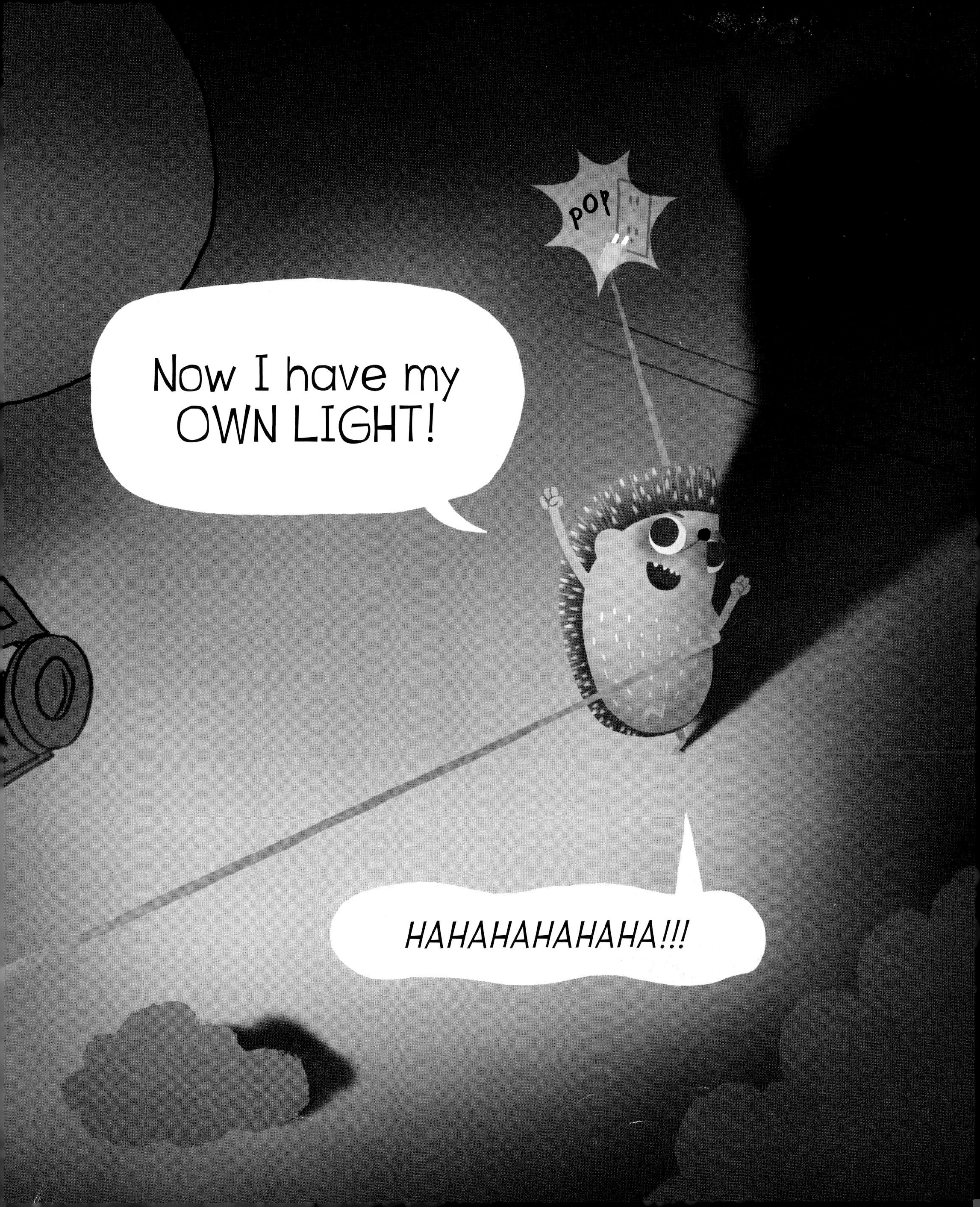
pop
Now I have my OWN LIGHT!
HAHAHAHAHAHA!!!

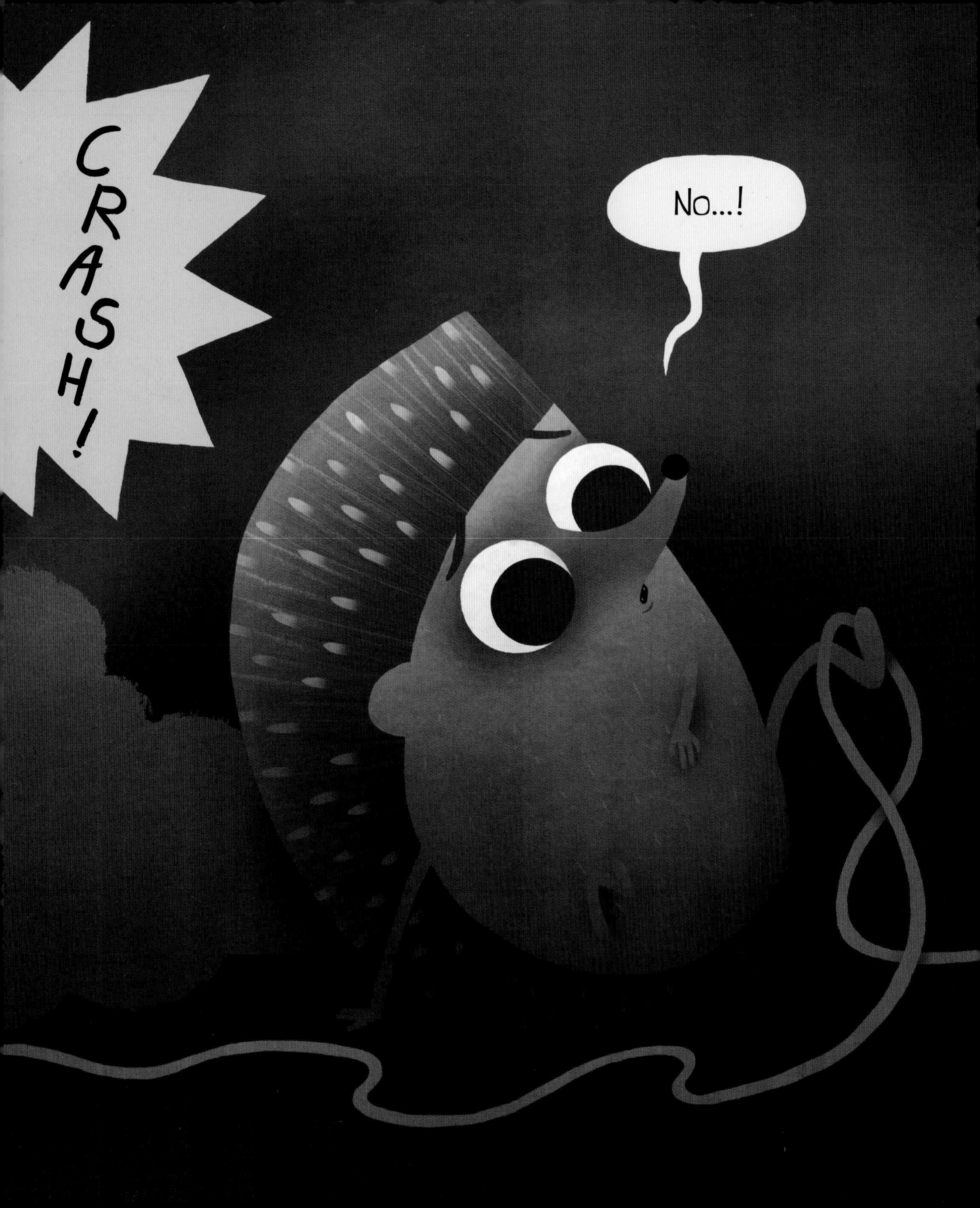
CRASH!
No...!

Ok. You win.

Just tell me...

Why are you
doing this to me?

click

Water?

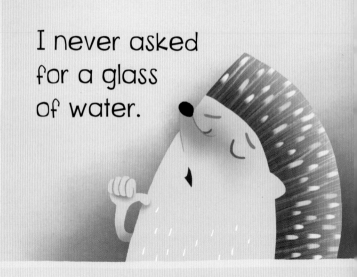

I never asked for a glass of water.

I did? Really?

I did. Huh.

Soooo... May I have it?

click

Umm...

I think I need to go
to the bathroom.